INFIDELIS

INFIDELIS

Vincent Cooper

MOUTHFEEL PRESS

Table of Contents

Origin

Decisions

Then: The Ultimatum — 1
The Coworker — 2
Pork Chop Platoon — 3
Smokey Bear — 8
Brothers — 11
9/11 — 13
Liberty — 15
Phonebooth — 16
Damian — 17
A Chicano During Wartime — 18
I Named You Starr — 20
Master Sergeant — 21
Brothers 2 — 22

Goodnight, Vietnam

Westside Ditty — 27
Amor — 28
An Unpopular War — 29
The Chicano Hero — 30
Infidelis — 31
Covers — 32
Final Wishes — 33
Goodnight, Vietnam — 34
British Evasion — 35
Veterano — 36
You're Not Gonna Make It — 37

Retrospect

Orans   41
Retrospect   43
Johnny   44
A Real Marine   46
The Call and Response   48
Bool-it Kachar   49
The Gimmick   50
Lyft Ride   52
Patriots?   53

Military In Hollywood

You Can't Handle the Truth   59
The Duality of Man   60
Errand Boys, Grocery Clerks and Bills   61
Napalm and Chorizo   62
An Ounce of Sweat Saves a Gallon of Blood   63
We Built This Bitch   64

Last Set

Barney Style   67
Gregg   68
Yearbook   69
Class of '98   70

Terms   75
Acknowledgments   77
Playlist   78
Author's Biography   79

This book is dedicated to Gregg Barrios—a queer author, playwright, teacher, columnist, book critic, poet, Veteran, and friend that I miss dearly.

&

Jim Marquez aka *Jimmy the Pen*, aka *The Beast*. Thank you for keeping it real and reminding us to write and put out our work fearlessly.

Origin

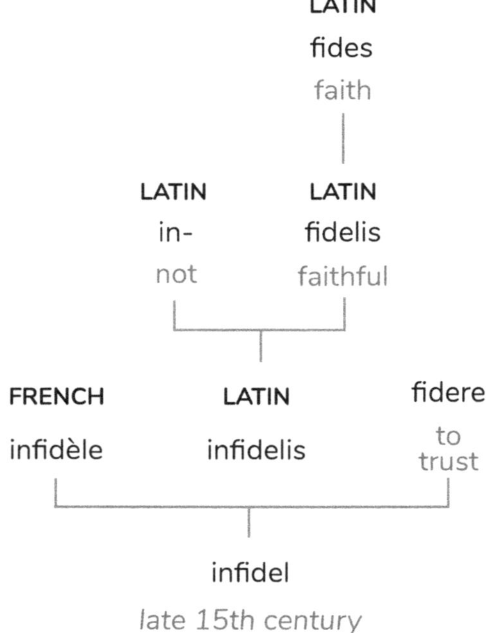

late 15th century: from French *infidèle* or Latin *infidelis*, from *in-* 'not' + *fidelis*, 'faithful' (from *fides* 'faith')

Decisions

Then: The Ultimatum

Let's get out of here.
My dad wants you out of the house
—or get a job so we can move out.
Go to the Army so we can have stability...
You'll be thin and sexy in a uniform—those dress blues.
We'll be able to travel—fuck Texas.

She pleads with me all the way to the recruiting station on Military Drive.

We park and argue for an hour.
Sailors in crackerjack and Marines in camouflage walk by hearing us
scream about where our relationship is going.

I had fallen in love with Carmen, who worked with me
at the downtown Marriott. I was a pool boy in aqua/khaki
and didn't have the balls to tell this teary Chicana in the car,
that I wanted to leave her.
I stare at her hard.

I pulled the door handle, bolted out
of the driver's seat of her father's ivory Sedan De Ville
and joined the United States Marines Corps.

The Coworker

At the hotel swimming pool
we hug tight, kiss softly,
glossy lips sweet like blood orange
staring into each other's eyes
while hotel residents smile at us walking by

Hey, I joined the Marines, I'll be leaving soon.

She holds on and says, "Take care of yourself"
places a love note written on hotel stationary in my khaki pocket—

the note perfumed (like her)—
smiley faces, lip prints and cursive lines of possibility.

When my shift was over, I tore it up, threw it away
called in sick the next day
and the next. . .then quit.
Broke up and made up with my GF.
Next day, we got married by the Justice of the Peace,

       her mother disgusted

         both of us trying to be happy

           disappointment on my recruiter's face.

The Pork Chop Platoon

Peacetime. That was the sell.

I

On the flight from San Antonio to San Diego,
recruits monologue *Full Metal Jacket.*
We pump each other up, laugh, doze off, and laugh again.
Looking out at the lights to the mountains,
we land.

An ivory school bus awaits,
we run in to sit, get told to duck our heads.
Inside, a drill instructor says,
Get your head up.
His face is like Son House.

In processing,
we civilians become *nasty recruits.*
Paperwork, clothing issued and regretting this decision,
I gotta take a shit but am afraid to ask,
wanting to go back home because *fuck this,*
waiting to be sorted into our platoon
after the first physical fitness test.
There are those who pass, move on to their platoon,
those who don't go to PCP.

II

Sitting in the sand, catching my breath the DI says,
You can't do one fucking pull up?
I jump back up, kipping...one...two
Stop kipping
Holding   p-u-l-l-i-n-g   three.
None of those count. You gotta be fucking kidding me.
Recruits who pass pridefully scream *YES SIR!*
Panting and confused
in a sloppy formation, drill instructors
scold like fathers, whispering insults
into ears of the rejected.
I glance at a plane in the sky flying away   from   here.
Shitbirds are rushed to a room with five payphones
on a brown brick wall.

Call your recruiter and tell him you failed.
Call your wife or mother and tell her, you'll graduate later.

My Chicano recruiter, thin-lipped, pencil-stached says,
Don't give up. Keep your head up.
My teenage bride says,
Just come home. It's okay.

III

Missing their girlfriends, boyfriends and family back home,

we are defeated. A drill instructor walks in, tells us,

this is home until we pass our test.

We need to lose weight
        recruiters make their quota
            train hard
                join a different platoon
                    to earn the title of Marine.

IV

In parade rest, Gomer Pyle sobs

to a Captain about quitting boot camp.

The officer breaks character

smirking, stating the consequences,

Dishonorable Discharge

Don't you want to be a Marine son?

Pyle's body nods.

At attention,

Captain tells me, "You shouldn't be here. I know you

can pass. Go back with the rest."

A walk of shame to the barracks where

PCP recruits mop the deck,

tighten their racks

spit-shine boots

put on cammies

march to the chow hall

to the diet of white rice and water.

No salt, pepper, or eye contact.

You're done

Then   we   run   run   run

falling out of formation like a welfare line

scattered, tired, fenced in from an airport and ocean.

V

In the recruit training handbook, there are pictures of drill instructors

showing how to disassemble your M-16 assault rifle,

clean it and reassemble it. You will shoot hundreds

of 5.56 MM rounds at a junk car; *King Kong ain't got nothing on me.*

A rubber male mannequin on swivels SMACK and back for more

a dog target at Camp Pendleton.

I don't remember anyone taking pictures

while rappelling down the side of a wall lettered:

M

A

R

I

N

E

S

or knocked out during pugil sticks.

There's no mention of PCP. Only the good times.

Smokey Bear

I

Clack-clack...clack-clack...clack-clack

I knew I would fuck it up

The heels of his corframs tread back and forth down the barracks.

(Tells recruits in low tone)

SMOKEY BEAR: Today, we will run faster. Feet will pivot better.
Knees will be chest high. No one will fall out of formation.
We will train. We will drill. We will be sharp. No mistakes.

[REVEILLE REVEILLE REVEILLE]

In the barracks of Charlie Company recruits roll out,

tighten their racks

four-inch fold

get dressed

by the numbers.

SMOKEY BEAR: 10-9-8-7-6-5-4-3-2-1 you are fucking done.

II

The Smokey Bears have been up for hours thinking of ways

to train sloppy, young civilians.

No more guzzling cokes on your couch, watching Monday Night Raw,

And your girlfriend is reading your love letters while *Jody*

is thrusting into her back home.

Missing home means being back on the block, smokin' and jokin',

Being a *shitbag* with your buddies

—a *nasty civilian.*

We miss it even more when the drill instructor's nails turn and twist

against our ribs to help make one more pull up.

Weeks of sixty second showers—

stinky men with their uncircumcised dicks swinging.

SMOKEY BEAR: *Double time. Up in the morning with the rising sun,
gonna run all day until the running's done.*

And we ran in green silk shorts,

      all of us here, west of the Mississippi,

          watching San Diego Palm trees swaying.

This was our alternative to get a job and get the fuck out

of mom's home…

III

Boot Camp started with an introduction of the Smokey Bears,
and ended at an Olive Garden with relatives staring at me,
asking how I felt. They said I looked great and where was I
going next. Pensively, I sipped water and told them I was
waiting on orders.

IV

At the end of "The Crucible" at Camp Pendleton, Smokey Bear said
he is proud of me. Placed an Eagle, Globe, and Anchor in the cup
of my hand, gave a brief biography, reminding me
of the times I told them I was leaving.

He calls me a Marine.

After wanting to leave the Marine Corp Recruit Depot
every single day, for months,
now having Italian McDonald's,
staring through the smiles of relatives,
I wanted to go back.

I was broken and this was home.

Brothers

All in all is all we are – Nirvana

His name was Fitz

His feet stunk up the room

All our eyes watered up

watching him peal green socks off

black toenails

He was from Seattle

and we bonded over Kurt Cobain.

Post high school,

Cobain was our Christ

and our generation

before September 11

only wanted to die.

We'd talk about the punk rock band we hadn't formed

and how we didn't fit the Marine Corps prototype:

- Dolph Lundgren, pointing an M-16 at the sky
- Muscles blasting out of a camouflage blouse
- Stone cold blue eyes
- Spikey blonde hair
- Dog tags resting on sweaty pecks

Fitz said,

I can't be here. I'm going UA. Go with me, man.

I laughed and walked with him to the entrance of the School of Infantry.

As soon as the gate opened

he said, *I'm running for it.*

To Oceanside, California:

water, sand, freeway and

non-judicial punishment—

he ran.

Twenty minutes later,

in an empty room a platoon sergeant winced,

held his aching knee and said,

"You two Hollywood Marines don't want to be here? I'm from *The Island* and my fellow Marine is my brother. Now, if you boys want to be here, get your ass out there and we'll forget about this."

Fitz, red-faced, said he was sorry,

he thanked me

for supporting him.

9/11

In San Antonio–on leave,

I turn on the 50-inch TV

It's a New York news channel, muted.

The coffee maker has roaches escaping

from molded coffee grains. I smash them

with my hand, wipe them off with my shirt,

roach legs remain stuck on me while the rest drop

to the floor. I clean out the coffee maker in the sink,

create a filter with napkins leftover from a taqueria.

In the cup, I pour expired Borden milk,

five spoons of sugar, brew Yuban coffee.

Sitting on the couch, I change the channel,

each station is showing the towers on fire,

then another plane collides into the World Trade Center.

People inside jumping out of windows

to their deaths.

I knew you shouldn't have joined;
Now you're going to war.

Called my tío in California,

the Vietnam Veteran laughs

and says, *You're not going to war. Call your recruiter.*

No answer.

After 9/11,

I fly into Palm Springs,

get taken by Corporal Macias

in a blue Volkswagen Beetle

to Twentynine Palms.

So, this is the fleet?

I am introduced to the Marines I will work with

as a Marine from PCP.

Are we going to war? I asked

No, not you.

Hey, but you made it right?

Liberty

A message from our Sgt Major:

Marines, be safe on this 72-hour liberty

We don't want phone calls from police officers to come bail you out

While on the golf course back 9

Also, don't get dead

Don't be on the news

Don't drink and drive like all those Marines that died last time

If you get a flat tire, replace it immediately

The donut spare is not a permanent tire

Think about what you're doing

Be safe

You are dismissed.

Phonebooth

Contreras walks into the room singing Shakira's "Dónde Están Los Ladrones"—on the floor, against the wall, I am staring at the phonebooth through the window up on a hill overlooking the base.
C: Why are you crying Coop?
V: I just fucked the girl next door. I cheated...I cheated on my wife.
C: No, pos, chingao, Coop. You don't gotta cry.
V: I gotta end it. I'm gonna call her and tell her it's over.
C: Maybe you should chill out. Listen to Shakira.
V: I'll be right back.

In the phonebooth, where barracks Marines sit all night talking
to partners, play guitar, sing love songs
J: Hello...What's up babe...you, okay?
V: I fucken cheated...I cheated on you. I'm sorry. I'm so sorry.
J: Who was it?
V: Some girl. I don't know her.
Dial tone.

Back to the barracks
Contreras hands me a Smirnoff Ice
We stay up singing "Moscas En La Casa"
Spit-shine our boots as he tells me about missing Laredo.
The girl next door walks in, whispers into my ear,
I'm married...I just thought you were hot. See you around.

Damian

A marriage counselor calls me an arrogant, immature Chicano from
Los Angeles and a drunk taking advantage of a young woman from
Texas. During the winter of Twentynine Palms, desolation inside a
desert, east of Palm Springs, she called to tell me we were pregnant
...divorce on hold for the hope of a newborn
She said, "When we have a son, we'll name him Damian." Plans were
made, bouncer/jumpers, toys, assembling cribs, onesies, chupetes, ah,
the cooing, the lavender baby soap.

A shifting within—
weeks later, a call that Damian was gone,
the Doctor said we can try to have another.
No response from me when a group of fellow Marines
enters the office.
One asks if I'm excited about the baby, I nod,
her whimper on the phone in my hand.
We apologize and hang up...like adults.
We lost the baby. D&C.
"Don't worry, this happens to everybody. She can still have kids."
But we're getting divorced.

A tumbleweed rolls by on a breezy afternoon.

Damian, my son, you'd be 20 years old now,
            just a whole other life we coulda had.

A Chicano During Wartime

I wanted to go to war
kill some time in Afghanistan
pick up Corporal
finalize my divorce
you know — out of sight   out of mind
lose some pounds
save money
breathe in the hot desert wind
and to know the stink of another country.

These boot marines
barely married
trying to sleep with brand-new wives
boot camp   S.O. I. get to the fleet
waiting all this time
now shipping out
and I wanted
to go to war
because too much American pop
too many movie scenes in my head
and Colonel Kurtz would be sitting on a sand dune waiting
for me, I'd tell him, I, too, am a poet.

A Chicano poet Marine de Califas
getting paper trailed outta the Marine Corps
pushed around and spit on by Staff Sergeants, Gunny's
daring me to take a swing.
This is what my tío meant
when he called me to say,
You're not gonna make it.

Afghanistan was not a war at first.
it was a business proposition.
Contracts, chess, checkers, choices, Cheney
—everyone wanted in.

The dive bars at home were filled with rednecks,
east coast Blacks and California Chicanos
—-all flirting with the same stripper.

The boot marines at home with new wives
working on pregnancy
hoping pity would let them stay
and I'm a drunk, hiding dope for friends
driving while intoxicated
volunteering to take their place.

Send me to the middle east
                             send me to die
in desert cammo's

                        just get me out of America

                                    I need a break.

Request denied–
you're staying here in Twentynine
liquored up and unauthorized absences...
a Sgt. looking for me
because I slept with his wife.

I Named You Starr

You were birthed by induction in September
almost missed the flight from Palm Springs to DFW.
Another session of hazing in the desert sun,
sand in my mouth, spitting it out, it was the end
of my time in the Marines.

You crowned thick brown hair, then a flash—
a nurse in blue scrubs handed me a clamp to cut
the umbilical cord.
The soft cry of new life was música,
temporarily mending wounds.

Your abuela told me,
It was time to grow up.
I nodded.

I wanted to be a father to you, instead
I became a faded name on a birth certificate,
your mother and I, along with
our hate, grew old.

She wrote Dallas on the name placard
because it was unisex
I named you Starr because you can say it in Spanish—
Estrella.

Master Sergeant

> *I want you out of my Marine Corps, you piece of shit,*
> *you can have your Honorable Discharge.*
> *We all know the truth, you'll be a hero to your kids, friends,*
> *and fat as a fucken house.*

I left Twentynine Palms in a brown Chevy Blazer:
No fight. No jailtime. Headed to Dallas, Texas.

Somewhere in the panhandle roadkill on the I-10 freeway—
armadillo upside down, an impaled deer
hunters in camouflage,
car windows rolled down,
wind too strong to chew, blowing away layers
of Marine camouflage—
government orders...
non-Judicial Punishment...
suspended male driver decals...
maxed out credit cards...
carbon copy D.U.I. tickets in the cupholder...,

the mirage of Master Sergeant smirking
in the rearview mirror. We lock eyes...
we all know the truth.
red lights flashing...
policeman signals me off the freeway,
writes up a speeding ticket.

Where ya headed?

Dallas.

Good luck, Devil Dog.

Brothers 2

Ten years later, in a dusty, storage box

a picture of me and Fitz

smoking Marlboro cigarettes.

A letter from the Department of the Navy:

Re: Period of Service Under Review

Cooper, Vincent P   Highest Rank: CORPORAL

Education Level: 12

MOS: 3432

-20010705: For on 20010703, SNM was UA from his appointed place of duty. SNM was caught by an NCO from the School of Infantry, as he and another Marine student left the land navigation course in an attempt to leave Camp Pendleton.

...To appeal this decision

...Get testaments from friends

...Coworkers, priests, or rabbis

...Evidence of sobriety

...Processing time fourteen months

I searched for Fitz on Facebook

for a testimony

to reconnect and reminisce.

No records found.

Goodnight, Vietnam

Westside Ditty

For my tío Rich and all the Chicanos in San Antonio
during the Vietnam War.

Go defend our country son, make Uncle Sam proud.
Don't worry about a High School Diploma,
You've got the Viet Cong to think about.

You'll be physically fit, cock strong, in your dress blues
All these westside girls are gonna want to fuck you

You'll have medals pinned on your chest, a career as a cook or custodian,
Benefits with a steady paycheck, a cheap little house with an iron fence.

C'mon be a real man with a rifle in your hands
And tell them all, later on, about the young heroes of war
Jungle sounds, Khe San and how things were in' Nam.

Amor

My tía met you while you were in R.O.T.C.

Then again at a Westside baile

"Talk to Me" played as you danced

True Chicano love

And a picture   maybe of

A teenage you and her

A mutual friend

And the devil from El Camaroncito.

An Unpopular War

Off to Vietnam

which was not Chicano,

it was not ancestral

to fight and kill people for political power

He was from San Anto—El Hueso

hungry for action   military city

heavily recruited gente to go eat the bullets

ingesting toxic orange and welcoming the fog

of jungles while rounds were constantly fired

as fellow Marines spoke about home where

coping with war was Chicano.

The Chicano Hero

"Hey Jude"
plays on a radio in Vietnam
when you are told you're going home.

The process: pack your uniforms, gear in the green seabag neatly,
black and white pictures of Marines, cigarettes in mouth, shirtless
and smiling, and a passport stamped "Okinawa, Japan."

The cold Pacific gently embraces crimson mountains
to Los Angeles International, then a shuttle down to San Diego
airport to San Antonio and no one to greet you.

You kiss the ground when you land, call a cab.

Hippies of the sixties protesting the war
keep "baby killer" in their mouths,
tight like the clothes in your seabag.

You strut on through.

The cab driver is one of the few to say
"Thank you for your service."
You don't remember his name.

At home, on the westside of San Antonio,
no welcome party,
just Dad watching T.V.,
no friends on the front lawn waiting with a beer

...Nothing

Infidelis

Full Metal Jacket is your favorite movie about Marine Corps bootcamp.
The accuracy of the Gunny and Gomer Pyle's rifle-in-mouth.
Guys at Pendleton jump the constantine-wired fence at night
run across the I-5 freeway and get hit by cars driving 80 miles per hour.
Others fall down hills to their deaths
so they won't have to become a Marine
or go to war.

Lots of suicide attempts, mi hijo.

Covers

I say oorah

You say OORAH

I say sir

You say SIR? I WORK FOR A LIVING

I say cap

You say MICKEY MOUSE WEARS CAPS. THIS IS A FUCKING COVER.

A MARINE CORP COVER.

Final Wishes

Thank you for your service
is what he wants to hear
from Chicanos, Blacks, Whites, Asians,
children and adults.

And when he dies
Tío wants to be planted face down
so the whole world can kiss his ass.

Goodnight, Vietnam

34

I am a father of six

I remain father hungry, collecting fathers as I go.

They are dying.

The men you served with, hold Trump-Maga-hats in the air,

spouting hate and violence...

To them I say,

Goodnight, Vietnam

There are no Marines in Aztlán.

British Evasion

Julian Lennon could never be

like his father

He did everything wrong

but wrote catchy pop songs to deal with Vietnam.

Veterano

Wearing a red and gold cover
that reads
    1967-1969 Reconnaissance USMC
raising a Devil Dog flag in the front yard
next to an American flag.

                  Everyone driving by knows
            who you are
        a Veterano
      for this country
    that is not yours
a dream you're not in.

You're Not Gonna Make It

You're not gonna make it, Tío said
He was the only consistent
father-figure I had
when I knew I wouldn't survive.

Tío went to 'Nam
recruiter snatched him up
like all recruiters in San Anto do,
round up gente to fight the wars of Euro juniors
to die for their red, white, and blue
on stolen indigenous land.

Tío came back to America,
a cook for the V.A.
Shit on Shingle,
best meal I ever had.

Retrospect

Orans

My father held me up to the ceiling
32 years old   drunkenly yelled   at relatives in the room
I am God. This is my son!

I don't remember looking at my family or
Mother apologizing for my dad.

It's 1984 and Mother grasps my arm
walks toward his
thick mustache, in Almansor Park—
stillness in the pine trees,
empty baseball diamonds,
a silent suite in tai chi poses.

Hello Paul, I say.
Call him Dad, he's your father, Mother says.

Paul sits on a field next to a jogging trail
Mother is at arm's length
soft words are spoken
I can't hear them, I'm playing
on the exercise equipment watching
their last kiss.

Paul rises slowly to assist my
four-year-old hands gripping the pull up bar,

struggling to hang on

Come on Vincent, pull...PULL

Hanging
losing my grip
finger by slippery finger
giant hands momentarily secure my ribs.
Blades of hair on each dorsal
pushing my body up
over the bar
grinning over at Mother.

We have to go, Mother says
in orans, distraught.

Mother cinches my elbow
marches   faster   away
glancing over my shoulder to
God's darkened frown.

In the backseat, Mother says
Count the palm trees
Until I fall asleep
each tree careening off the car window.

Retrospect

4th grade Teacher, 1989

What do you want to be when you grow up Coop?

I don't know.

Come on. Do you want to be a Fireman? Police Officer?

Can I tell the weather like Dallas Raines?

The meteorologist on TV?

Yes, I want to grow up and have cool hair and toss it around while telling everyone what the weather is.

Co-Worker, 2000

A Marine? You hate the government and George Bush. Why would you choose to protect him? To be a fucking robot? You're crazy.

12-year-old daughter, 2015

Dad, can I have all your Marine uniforms?

You can have my cammies. They don't fit anymore.

Retrospect, 2020

I shoulda been a Chicano weatherman in Southern California.

Johnny

"Momma told Johnny not to go downtown, Marine Corps Recruiter
was hanging around."

My stepson says he wants to be a Marine like me.
A Marine like me. A Marine...LIKE ME.

You're not going to hack it, I say.
You can't even wake up at 6 AM,
there's no urgency in your body,
you're not ready,
just go to college
be an engineer for NASA.

Your grandma wants you to fight
for Trump and Jesus Christ,
to settle you down and make a man out of you.
You're not going to make it, and I'll be damned
if you come home on a Greyhound bus
with a Dishonorable Discharge forever.

I won't let you down, he says.
Yes, you will.
This isn't the same Corps,
you can try to be an airman like your bio-dad.
There's no way you'll survive the Marines,
you won't even make it past the scale at MEPS.

He pushes his portholes up the bridge of his nose.
His cold stare directed at me.

18 years ago,
I picked up the phone,
to hear my tío say,
I heard you want to be jarhead.
Mi hijo, you're not going to make it,
you'll never be able to hack it
I know you and your personality,
you won't make it.
I know I can't stop you.
Stop eating tacos and start working out
and let me know how it goes

Yes sir.

One day,
at 2 AM,
while we were sleeping,
Johnny left us for a girl,
and Zennial freedom.

A Real Marine

is physically fit

says OORAH when they see another Marine

has American pride

honors the Eagle, Globe, and Anchor

has a bulldog named Chesty

tells war stories while polishing his medals

banks with USAA

psycho tough

ready to kill

never hesitates

knows martial arts like Chuck Norris

is an alcoholic with a side fling

has PTSD

a racist in denial

attends air shows with the Silent Drill Platoon

A real Marine thinks this country has gone to shit
Doesn't want to die because his grandson is gay
On the flip, he wants gays in the military to serve
as bullet-catchers

A real Marine gets shafted by the Corps
years later, wears a red cover USMC t-shirt
won't stop until the job is done

has flashbacks

haircut high n' tight

originates from Parris Island

is sometimes a tío taco

is not that amphibious

a cock boy in dress uniform

who marches at grocery stores

A real Marine

trains people of color

to kill people of color

A real fucking Marine

trains to kill anyone, anything

even himself.

The Call and Response

48

> "And If I die in a combat zone
> Box me up and ship me home
> Put me in a set of Dress Blues
> Comb my hair and shine my shoes
> Pin my medals upon my chest
> Tell my momma I did my best.
> Mama mama don't you cry, Marine Corps motto is do or die."

Millions of skulls in the dirt, sand and oceans of Earth

    do not sing *do or die*

They would rather be alive, looking into their loved one's eyes

    but the reality of war has eroded them

Population control

    is the killing business of humanity

The rich white are in the killing business

    and business is good.

Bool-it Kach-er

1. Is any member of the military in the Department of Defense.

2. A white person that dies for White America. See Patriot.

3. A derogatory term given to Marines to mock "First to Fight" slogan "send in the Marines to fight and die first, let the Army clean up the rest."

4. A reject within the Marine Corps such as a person who cannot keep up in formations, drill, physical training.

5. A person not worthy of being a Marine but worthy of catching bullets for another Marine during war time.

6. A person of color and LGBTQ+ in the military because they are a person of color and LGBTQ+. See DADT.

7. A victim from being shot by the police who are former military personnel who have PTSD.

8. Someone who is in the wrong place and wrong time during war. or a crime.

The Gimmick

Chicano brothers and sisters,
I WANT YOU
to take back what is ours,
this land is your land
this land is Aztlán.

Daddy wears Marine Corps gear
red and gold pride
do or die
He wants you to be a man
get a G.I. Bill
make your time worth it
get all the benefits
try not get married
don't have kids
just live it up
look sharp
uniform starched
sharp creases
stiff walk
clack the heels
from your spit-shined Cadillac's.

The Marines tell you
we're all green for equality
we fight for honor
we die for freedom
so Americans can watch American Idol
with a Budweiser on the arm of their couches
and their children be glued to iPad apps
Maga 2.0.

Later, you hear your Brown Marine brother
is being deported
and you vouch for him
tell Facebook that he is a hero
while our government says
Thank you for being a front-line bullet catcher
now go back to Mexico.

Your son who followed your footsteps says
It's a thankless job I shoulda chased
that woman I loved
or the job in L.A. that I wanted.

Lyft Ride

52

"Tomorrow who's gonna fuss?"

The Replacements

The middle-aged Army veteran says:

> *I got no problems with trans in the military*
> *but in the moment of truth*
> *they just won't shoot.*
> *They're only here for a college degree...*
> *Can't trust them to protect our country,*
> *because their core isn't to kill.*
> *On the battlefield, with pants soaked in piss...*
> *Talkin' about a college degree...*
> *In the Army, we have crackheads asking to delay their urinalysis.*

Recalibrate your code [Primogeniture]

Your grandfathers   roaming guilty   in the ghost world

can't hurt you

or keep you   in the closet   anymore.

Recalibrate your code [Primogeniture]

Do BIPOC this favor

We want to see our non-binary grandchildren grow.

Patriots?

Look, no one cares if you hate the Marine Corps
Or regret joining
No one cares if you're suicidal or PTSD
It doesn't matter if you become a nasty civilian
Fat as a house
Or a punk with makeup on
Or some anti-marine anarchy

The day they put that Eagle, Globe and Anchor in your hand
You earned the title of Marine.
You'll always be gang fucking green.
Always one of us.

Never EX.

Military in Hollywood

You Can't Handle the Truth

~Jack Nicholson in A Few Good Men

Reimagine natural birth as you enter Earth

copal-scented-

       tears bring smiles from those who love you

Brown toes step on dirt and chaparral

a mother nurses

       a father serves

Learn of ocean, sun, and moon,

the thousands of

            stars, ancestors, Nahuatl —

               no pledge of allegiance

Seeds in the cup of Brown hands

food is natural

       the plucking and pulling

             blue sky is a friend

Corazón, amor y vida

animal brother/ fire sister

         no one fears death

           as it is only next

No one needs a military

         if one's soul is at peace.

The Duality of Man

60

~Matthew Modine in *Full Metal Jacket*

Jesus H. Christ
Chicanos are not killers
they are chameleons
Jung was not a Chicano
born to kill is a motto of kill culture

One must have decorum even in the coldness of murder
wipe off the blood
erase the prints
have composure post death.
The murdered must die gracefully
for the sake of a Hemingway
the literati will forever praise the death
and the way the death was writ.

A conflict of power volunteering the poor to die for the rich
risking deportation versus The American Wars
People of color killing people of color

The wealthy 1% must kill all the ones below
even if some of them are their own.

Errand Boys, Grocery Clerks and Bills

~Marlon Brando in *Apocalypse Now*

You're nothing—remember that.

no gold medals

no purple hearts

no certificate on parchment

no silver badges

no kill culture honor

can take away the people of color killed

labeled as enemies of your country

You see the dead in your dreams

and the dead want to kill you back—

memories in plaque and white

Not enough booze and cigarettes to soothe

your obsession with men and guns

and you wake up staring at the ceiling

with blood on the left hand a knife in the right

Rinse repeat

you take your kids to Disney

everything looks like a fucking VC

What's behind door #3?

PTSD.

Napalm and Chorizo

62

~Robert Duvall in *Apocalypse Now*

I love the smell of chorizo in the morning

sizzling with diced onions and jalapenos:

smells like home

the 80's and abuelos.

Napalm smells like

no home

no grandparents

only charred bodies, smoking trees

and grass burning.

The confederates want you to cheer for them

because some day

some sweet day their war will end

and there will be no one else to kill

but themselves.

Ounce of Sweat Saves a Gallon of Blood

Inspired by Patton's speech

Remember Blacks and Mexicans
go hard or die
war is a money maker
Someone (not you) gets all the money, land and power
but you will die in the mud face down
at a beach while not on vacation
in a jungle so humid your corpse will sweat
a burning city and you can make your boss
proud by killing enough.

The harder and faster you kill
the quicker you'll get home to a sofa
and your old lady while your kids playing
with toys in front of a big screen TV
remind you of the enemy children you captured,
imprisoned or killed
with no hesitation.

Post War
Holding a frame with a picture of you before the murdering
locked into a smile
then, the sound of ammunition rounds.

We Built This Bitch

~Chad Boseman in *Da 5 Bloods*

Chicanos, Chicanas, Afro-Latino/a, Black, Indigenous
We built this bitch.
We are not a kill culture.
We even sing the songs of slave traders with soul.

We built America from tracks to streets
brick and mortar to corporations.
It's our blood, sweat, and tears on the soil,
hanging from trees,
shot in the streets,
blood on concrete.

We built America through Manifest Desmadre
Let's take it back. It is ours.
Unite!
Do not enlist.
Love yourselves and live your lives.
Stop trying to survive.

There are not enough reparations to balance out the murdering.

Last Set

Barney Style

Son, don't ya understand now?

~Springsteen

After further review, no G.I. Bill for you
Upgrade denied, again
If you disagree with the board's decision
present a new case with new evidence
keep in mind you're 40 years' old
and fighting this fight
for more benefits
a better reputation
is becoming more and more pathetic.

Re-read the PDF of your time in the Marines
it's all there in black and white
you were a good Marine
with a decent PFT score
but the higher ups hated you
drank too much
fraternized
You wanted us to become one of you
instead of you becoming one of us
In the end
you rot and die
We win. That's it.
Carry on.
Don't say Oorah; It's not a Chicano word.

Gregg

Pienso en ti
esta mañana, en un mundo
sin ti

Pienso de Crystal City
David Bowie y Lou Reed
y tu tiempo en Vietnam.

Desayuno tacos y café
hablo de un viaje a Los Angeles.

Pienso en ti
y los regalos de libros
tu amplia sonrisa
de todos los autores que son personas de color

Que te pases bailando
con La Nico en un jardín
diciendo que vida tan loca

Arte y tiempo
Al rato, vato

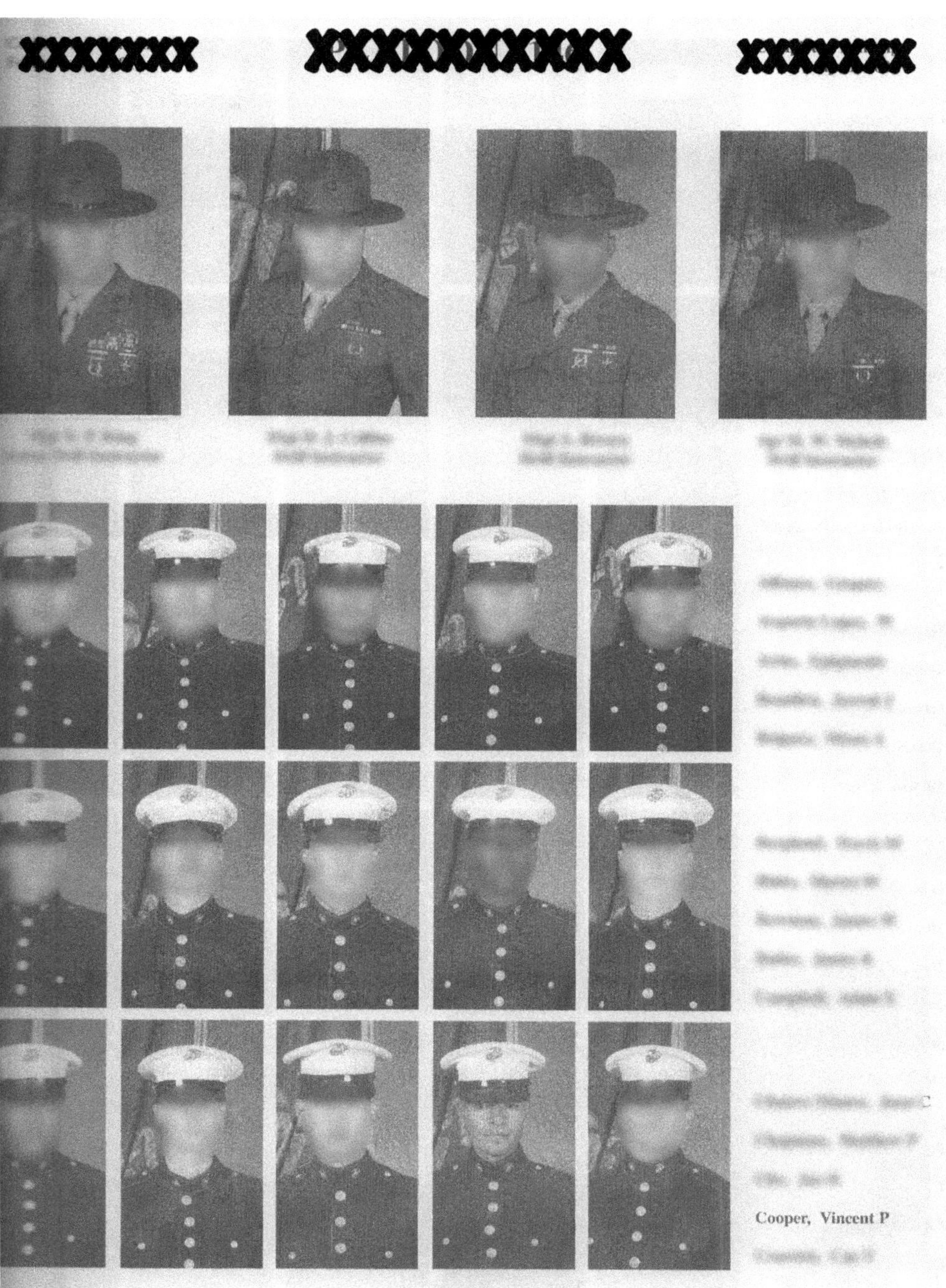

Cooper, Vincent P

Class of '98

I

After graduation, the question was
What's next?
UNLV Runnin' Rebels or general population?
Smoke-filled casinos, slot machines bing-binging
coin slot credit and the whiff of dry Vegas heat.
Neon lights and a post nervous breakdown promises to get
back to California Palm Trees and cold beaches to write
screenplays. Left mother at a filthy Vegas Greyhound Bus station
waving and crying. Went through jobs like changing
underwear: Edison Electric, Eastmont Intermediate
and the tiendita next door. Filled my spiral notebooks
with poems in a room with a blue light bulb and the underwear
drawer held stolen bottles of El Presidente,
Lou Reed's Coney Island Baby on repeat.

II

Chente never brought a girl home, he must be a joto.
Cue A-O-L dial-up tone and cousins sign me up to chat
and meet women on the internet.
Listen man, you need a driver's license, car, apartment, and job.
These are four basic things you need in life.

III

I was poor, and women my age wanted college prep guys
Tattooed chipster mechanic, I was awkward
wearing black corduroy pants, black chuck's, blue fleece,
shades and the beginning of a drinking problem.

Then, a Southside San Antonio Chicana replied, "Hey what's up,"
chatting became chisme, then calling cards
and sitting in a phone booth reading poems to her.
Los Necios.

IV

"I'm gonna move to San Antonio to be with you."
She said, "Don't move here. This is not the place for you."
Friends said, "Don't leave. She's not good enough for you."
I moved.

Arriving in San Antonio,
brother greets me, humidity, and a ride straight
to her house. Front door opens. Walking in
I see her sister laid out on the couch watching MTV.
She's standing in the middle of the living room.
"Why are you here? I told you not to."
All the conversations of love were gone
I can't believe you moved here...
There's nothing for you here.

V

A relationship of nothing
Sound tracked by freestyle music
Drawn eyebrows and lip liner
Living for Sunday night
Cruising down Military drive
My spikey blonde hair tips
Working as a pool boy
Neck, covered in hickeys

VI

A year later, ready to call it quits
never enough money
hard luck stories
couldn't buy a house or get established
didn't sell drugs
just your regular 40-hour work week.
Her father worked in car upholstery
offered me to work with him as a go for learn
the family business but I stayed in the room
wrote poetry on buses
of Westside and Southside San Antonio
worked minimum wage

"My dad wants you out of here," she said.
Me too.
Bridges were burning, fake apologies, money – not saved.
No stability.

A lost
      post high school
            teen of the 90's

Grabbed the keys, got in the car, she stood in the street.
"Where are you going?"
C'mon...get in.

Marine Terms

PCP – Physical Conditioning Platoon is an alternate platoon for Recruits who fail their initial test when arriving at boot camp and placed in remedial training.

PCP – Pork Chop Platoon, when Marines who did not fail their initial test and mock the recruits who did.

Shitbirds – a reject, outcast, dud, civilian not good enough to be a Marine.

Jody – name for male who is sleeping with your significant other while you worry about her during your bootcamp blues. Also, Jody or Jodie when Drill Instructors sing while marching with their platoon.

Gomer Pyle – television show from 60's, Vincent D' Nofrio's character in *Full Metal Jacket*.

Recruit – is a person who has not yet earned the title of Marine.

Cammies – camouflage blouse/pants.

Rack – bed

By the numbers – is a countdown you are given by Drill Instructors to complete a task.

Smokin' and jokin' - is referred to as the days prior to bootcamp hanging out with your friends as an undisciplined civilian.

MCRD San Diego – All Recruits west of the Mississippi are sent to bootcamp in San Diego.

MCRD Parris Island – All Recruits east of the Mississippi River are sent to South Carolina.

NJP – Non-Judicial Punishment is when you're reprimanded but not in a court of law.

Fleet – term for your actual job/MOS after graduating bootcamp and technical school.

Boot Marines – brand new Marines.

S. O. I. – School of Infantry.

Devil Dog – nickname for Marine who fought at Belleau Wood. "Teufel Hunden."

SNM – said name Marine.

NCO – Non-commissioned officer

El Camaroncito – legendary dance hall where the devil once appeared and danced with our abuela's in San Antonio, TX.

El Weso or El Hueso – means the Westside of San Antonio.

Agents of Orange – lyrics from Rage Against the Machine's "Sleep Now in the Fire."

Veterano – Veteran of the department of defense or Chicano from the streets.

Aztlán – the land that the majority of people call America.

Cadillac's – nickname for boots that are spit-shined.

Barney Style – explaining to a person in slow terms or to dumb it down for someone to understand. Let me break it to you Barney style.

Acknowledgements

Versions of these poems from Infidelis have been published in *Somos En Escrito, Huizache, The Acentos Review, Dryland Lit, Boundless Anthology, Riversedge Journal, Good Cop/Bad Cop Anthology, Contra–Texas Anthology, Abstract Magazine, Barrio Panther*.

Film Quotes and Credits:

A Few Good Men. Director: Rob Reiner, written by Aaron Sorkin. Castlerock/ Columbia 1992

Full Metal Jacket. Director: Stanley Kubrick, written by Stanley Kubrick, Michael Herr, Gustav Hasford. Natant, Harrier Films. Warner Bros (U.S) Columbia-Cannon (UK) 1987

Apocalypse Now. Director: Francis Coppola, written by Francis Coppola and John Milius. Omni Zoetrope, United Artists 1979

Patton. Director: Franklin J. Schaffner, written by Francis Coppola and Edward North. 20th Century Fox 1970

Da Five Bloods. Director: Spike Lee, written by Danny Bilson, Paul De Meo, Kevin Willmott and Spike Lee. 40 Acres and a Mule, Filmworks, Rahway Road, Lloyd Levin/Beatriz Levin Production, Netflix 2020.

Music Quotes/References – Bad Religion, Sunny Ozuna, Bruce Springsteen, The Beatles, Nirvana, Talking Heads, Son House, Marine Corps Cadences/ Jodies, Danny Brandt, The Replacements, Lou Reed, David Bowie, Nico, Freestyle, Rage Against the Machine.

Thank you to:

Viktoria Valenzuela, Mouthfeel Press, Richard Ramon Sr, Mike Rivas Jr., Gregg Barrios, Edward Vidaurre, Jose B. Gonzalez, Adrian Ramon, Beatrice Rivas, Jacinto Guevara, César De Léon, Christopher Martinez, J. Villanueva, José Angel Araguz.

Special thanks to artists Jacinto Guevara and Cayetano Valenzuela.

Playlist

Song Credit: Greg Graffin. "We're Only Gonna Die." Epitaph Records, 1982.

Song Credit: Joel Senecas. "Talk to me." King Records, 1958

Song Credit: Bruce Springsteen. "Born in the U.S.A." Columbia Records, 1982

Song Credit: Lennon-McCartney. "Hey Jude." Apple, 1968

Song Credit: Kurt Cobain. "All Apologies." DGC, 1993

Song Credit: Paul Westerberg. "Androgynous." Twin/Tone 1984

Song Credit: Greg Graffin. "You Don't Belong." Epitaph 2001

Song Credit: Mebarak-Ochoa. "Dónde Están Los Ladrones." Columbia, Sony Latin 1998

Song Credit: Shakira. "Moscas en la Casa." Sony Latin 1999

Song Credit: Lou Reed. "Coney Island Baby." RCA 1975

Vincent Cooper is the author of the chapbook *Where the Reckless Ones Come to Die*, published by Aztlan Libre Press in 2014, and a full-length poetry collection, *Zarzamora: Poetry of Survival* published by Jade Publishing in 2019. Cooper co-edited the anthology, *Good Cop/Bad Cop*, published by Flowersong Press in 2021. His poetry can be found in *Huizache*, AMP Hofstra University's *Digilit Magazine*, *Riversedge Journal*, *Somos En Escrito*, *Dryland Lit*, Latinoliteratures.org, *Abstract Magazine*, Digging Press *Poetry Series 2022*, *Voices de la Luna*, *La Voz de Esperanza*, *The Acentos Review*, and Labloga.blogspot.com. Cooper is a member of The Macondo Writers Workshop, selected in 2015. He currently resides in southside San Antonio with his wife and poet Viktoria Valenzuela and their children.